Heaven's Entry Lube Park

Timothy L. Edwards

Contents

In The Beginning

And in the beginning God created the heavens and the earth. Many, many years later, he decided to build a lube park on Earth. We, being Enya Deep and Justin Alittle, were unwittingly drafted by God himself, perhaps with some input from his famous son, to make His lube park a reality.

Enya recalled being in the middle of an erotic dream that night when he was startled by a bright light and a booming voice. The voice commanded Enya to build a lube park. It had to be on exactly sixty-nine acres, no more, no less, and it had to be Bible themed. Enya vividly remembered the end of his erotic dream and the interruption by God. Both would be important recollections when the lube park plans were being developed.

After he awoke, Enya called his best friend Justin to share the news of his dream.

"Hey Justin, you will not believe the vivid dream I had last night!"

" I probably would. Did it involve sex?"

"Well, yes, initially it did, but that's not all. God appeared and told me to build a lube park. He even included very specific details. The park has to be built on 69-acres, and be Bible themed. "

"Hahahahahaha. Uh huh. You mean a water park?"

"No. A LUBE PARK. I know that lube was mandatory, although not explained why. At the end of the dream I recall saying, 'Jesus I am coming', so I think that means I agreed to build the park. After that I woke up. Stop by later. We have a lot of work to do. We have been called upon by God Himself to do His work."

As if by a miracle, Enya had a vision later that morning. Within that vision the name of the park was revealed to him. As Enya sat upon the toilet, the words "Heaven's Entry Lube Park" flashed before him. "We shall build that lube park, and it shall be good", he thought.

Enya and Justin met later that day. They understood and accepted their divine calling. Therefore the men worked thereafter for weeks on the park plans. They bought sixty-nine acres in the U.S. Bible belt. The men planned rides, restaurants, bars, themes, gifts shops, snacks, drinks, shops, entertainment, and games. They contacted amusement park ride designers, local construction companies, and church leaders. They thought of everything (they hoped) one would need for a Bible themed park using lube instead of water. God commanded and the men obeyed.

Enya hoped that God would appear again to explain the importance of lube to the park. Wouldn't water be sufficient he wondered? Or maybe God would appear on opening day. Much to his disappointment, God never again visited Enya or the park. Maybe He lost interest in the lube park and moved on to healing crippled children or ensuring his favorite team won a sporting event. Who knows? He is God after all and can do whatever He wants to do, whenever He wants to do it. No one is allowed to question His motives. But Enya was inspired by the word of God, and made it his calling to build the park. Enya believed that God would bless the lube park, (appearance or not) making it profitable.

Several months later the park was becoming a reality. Contractors worked on the 69-acres to construct God's dream lube park. Enya, being a wise man, held back nineteen acres for the Sisters of the Lord Resort and Casino.

Three years from the day Enya's dream occurred, Heaven's Entry Lube Park opened its doors to the public. A large north star affixed atop a 150-foot tower led people to the $30 per-car parking lot. Hundreds of people traveled from all across the world that opening day. Wise men, monks, priests, ministers, faith healers, rich, poor, men, women, and children, all stood in line for their chance to be one of the first to visit the new park. The first ticket holder to enter the park exclaimed "Praise Jesus!" and then she quickly proceeded to the Tubing for Jesus lazy river ride.

Park Entry, Rules, and Information

As guests drive up to the park, they are greeted by life size cut-outs of Bible favorites, pointing them to the parking attendant booths where $30 per car is collected. Guests marvel at the North Star atop a 150-foot tower which guided them to God's inspired lube park. Well, realistically the North Star and Google maps more than likely guided them.

Atop the golden entry gates are the words ``Heaven's Entry Lube Park" each letter being 15-cubits tall, gold in color, and adorned with Angels. The entry is breathtaking and sets the tone for the fun family day at the park.

Adjacent to the ample parking area is the Heavenly Paws Pet Resort and a Faith Healing Chapel.

On each Parking Booth and each ticket sales booth, guests will see the park's ten commandments posted:

I. Have a good time. Relax and enjoy! We don't judge. (Truth be known as a Biblically themed park, of course we judge. At the end of each day, all park employees meet and judge, shame, and generally disparage multiple guests. The Roman guards play snippets of video tapes of guests for cvcn more judgmental hilarity.)

II. Public nudity has been shunned since that whole apple thing back in the day. Clothes and swimsuits will be modest. Fig leaf clothing, sewn by local church ladies, is available for purchase in the various gift shops. If a guest is clothing shamed, he/she will be required to purchase fig leaf clothing, or be escorted from the park by the Roman guards (security).

III. Lube makes everything in the park fun, but slippery! Use the hand rails.

IV. No pets or wheelchairs allowed. If a guest needs a pet for emotional support or due to a disability, they should visit the faith healer adjacent to the ticket booths. If the faith healer cannot cure the guest, then feel free to board your animal at the Heavenly Paws Pet Resort next to the faith healer's chapel.

V. Obey the Roman Guards at all times. Their swords may be fake, but they will not fake removing sinners from the park. Consistent with the practices of the various religions, park management decides by its own subjective manner what is sinful and what isn't.

VI. The general park restrooms are separated by gender. "Holy Shit" (Men) and "Angel's Relief" (Women). In the food court, the restrooms are identified as "Banana" (Men) and "Split" (Women). The locker rooms are identified as Adam for men and Eve for women.

VII. Due to unfortunate circumstances, the park's legal team would not allow the park to maintain the private family restroom. So please plan to use gender assigned restrooms.

VIII. The park only uses environmentally friendly water-based lube (tested and approved by the LGBTQ community). Guests are encouraged to shower at the end of their visit to remove all lube. A change of clothing is recommended.

IX. Wives must obey their husbands and children must obey their parents while in the park. Absolutely no coveting of other guests is permitted. (See rule V.)

X. Oh be careful little lips what you say. As guests enter the park, they must put these all away: anger, wrath, malice, slander, and obscene talk.

Park Information

- Guests pay $69 each for a ticket, which includes a small map of the park. There is no discount for seniors or children because regardless of age we are all God's children.

- Reed stroller rentals available for a deposit of $19 and a daily rental rate of $69.

- Wheelchairs are not available. The faith healing chapel is conveniently located for all who may profess to require the necessity for a wheelchair. If the visit to the faith healer does not cure the guest, the Park believes it is God's will that the guest not be permitted to attend his lube park. Alternatively, guests who believe in the power of the Lord should purchase and apply "The Lord Works In Mysterious Ways Fruity Healing Lube", to the afflicted body part for a potential miraculous healing. All of our lube is blessed and holy.

- Heaven's Entry Lube Park is a haven for all, near and far, who want to experience the slippery joy of lube with their park activities. Guests do not need to be Bible lovers to enjoy all the park has to offer. Join us for slippery fun.

- For guests needing medical attention, the park's medical clinic, "Let's Play Doctor" is available. Staffed by volunteers from local churches, these church ladies are sure to cure what ails you. (Full disclosure, the volunteers receive season passes for two as compensation for their service to the ill park guests.)

- Let the little children come to me, and do not hinder them, for the Children of the Lord Daycare belongs to such as these. Do not let the little children suffer because the park operates the Children of the Lord Daycare for the little tots who need a break from the fun. Hourly rates. Ages birth to eight. Age-appropriate Bible studies.

- Season passes available. Show your clergy card and receive a discount.

- Each day the park staff maintains over 500,000 gallons of lube for park rides and attractions. Most of the valves are operated manually, hands-on. Our maintenance men enjoy a good hand job as opposed to having the equipment operated automatically.

- Adam and Steve, a local architect firm, designed a 30-seat chapel for guests to enjoy during their day at the park. In their honor, the park named the chapel The Adam and Steve Garden of Eden Chapel. Available for weddings!

- The park owners plan to expand by adding the Sisters of the Lord Resort and Casino. Stay tuned for announcements as the world's only Bible themed casino is built on the park's undeveloped south acreage.

The Rides and Attractions

The park design team included amusement park ride designers from all over the world. The rides include family rides, kid rides, and thrill rides. Something for everyone. Most rides are based on Biblical themes. Rides not based upon Biblical themes were designed to thrill the guests and bring them closer to Jesus. Say your prayers and hop on!

Our attractions are state-of-the-art! Designed with one idea in mind, FUN! Sit and relax at one of our shows, try your luck at the carnival games, or kayak across our lake to tour the God dam, built by our lone beaver.

Holy Roller

Holy Roller rivals any existing rollercoaster. Our roller coaster doesn't dance or roll on the floor but it does shake-rattle-n-roll along the track. Riders can practically see heaven as the cars move up the track at a petrifying 45-degree angle before reaching the 150-foot peak. Riders say their prayers as the cars speed like hell down the steep drop.

At the bottom of the drop the coaster gains speed and hurls the riders through the Holy Trinity, a series of three intense loops. It almost feels like the holy trinity (three distinct loops) form one larger loop as the riders are whipped around.

The coaster cars then dive into the long, hot, dark tunnel nicknamed the Pits of Hell. The tunnel temperature is maintained at 100 degrees. From there the cars slow down as they approach the golden gates, signaling the end of the ride.

"I loved the intensity of the holy trinity loops. It was a spiritual experience that ultimately hyper-extended my neck. It's a small price to pay to honor my savior though. " Austin T. from Houston, Texas.

Pope on the Slippery Slope

One of our most popular thrill rides is the Pope on the Slippery Slope. The Pontiffs will tempt you to try your skills on a surfboard adorned with realistic painted pictures of the last five pontiffs. Try to stay upright as the pontiffs stare up at you. Don't let the pontiff's stares distract you though!

Will you fall and be swept away as the lube rushes below you at 60mph? To avoid falling, less skilled or nervous surfers enjoy sitting on the face of a pontiff for the duration of the ride.

"I wanted to learn to surf so I tried the Pope on a Slippery Slope ride. All I managed to do was sit on the Pontiff's face for 10-minutes. Still, it was a good time." Maria G. from Butte, Montana

"When I told my mom I spent 10-minutes sitting on Pope Paul's face, she slapped me. After I explained about the Pope on the Slippery Slope ride, we both laughed. What a great day at the park for a teen. Thanks mom." Billy Bob Jr. from Texarkana, Arkansas

Cardinal Sin

It takes a park to raise a child. Therefore, the Cardinal Sin merry-go-round is a must have for any legitimate Bible park. Kiddos will enjoy sitting on a six-foot ceramic replica of a cardinal bird. The cardinal's merry-go-round slowly circles as the birds chirp out Bible verses addressing cardinal sins, designed to scare the children into behaving.

Park employees dressed as Catholic Cardinals or Rabbis will frequently walk amongst the spinning guests, casting glares of disapproval.

"My child was traumatized on the Cardinal merry-go-round. We are atheists and the beautiful red cardinal scared him to believe he was a sinner. The Bible Thumpers show was really nice." Ruth P. from Jerome Arizona.

"Our entire family enjoyed the merry-go-round. The short rabbi was scary and Cardinal Frank had a frightening stare. I think the kids learned a lesson about sinning. Thank you for the amazing experience and help with the kids." Gilbert from Auburn, Michigan.

Tubing for Jesus

For guests who just want to relax, Tubing for Jesus is the perfect choice. Guests enjoy a relaxing trip around the park sitting on a life size Jesus float tube with his loving arms wrapped around them.

Buckled in Jesus' arms for safety, the riders will enjoy a lazy trip around the park in a river of 60,000 gallons of our sunscreen and healing lube. (No sunburns here.)

Gladys of Centralia, Illinois, was so inspired she felt she could leave tube Jesus behind and walk on the lube's surface. But the rule is to stay seated and secured in Jesus arms. Thankfully Gladys obeyed.

"Tubing for Jesus was amazing! When the ride attendant strapped Jesus' loving arms around me, I felt something inside me. I found out later what I was feeling was pain because the arms were strapped on too tight. The Lube was cool and soothing though. I would highly recommend this ride for those who do not like to walk all day." Clara C. from Redfield, South Dakota.

“My tube had a leak which caused Jesus’ hands to fall down onto my lap. Other floating guests looked away in shame because the arms of their fully inflated Jesus were appropriately placed. I enjoyed his loving arms! I laughed so hard I almost peed myself. Most fun I have had in years!” Rashid from India.

Lube the Disciples

Lube The Disciples is the ultimate choice for those who want to slip and slide down an extra slippery slope. On this ride, guests will walk through the lube tube where they will be sprayed with a generous amount of Holy Lube (available for sale in the gift shops) prior to reaching the launch area. The guests will then run and jump on a slip-n-slide, built on the side of a 100-foot hill, emptying into a lube pool. The slip-n-slide is covered with pictures of the Disciples.

Guests sometimes complain that they are unable to see the picture of their favorite disciple, because they hurl along so quickly! We remind them that the gift shop does have a video of the Lube the Disciples ride which clearly shows each Disciple; available for $49.99.

"I cannot believe how fast I slid down the Lube the Disciples slide! It was amazing, yet scary. Lube definitely makes the ride much faster than water. Slippery clean fun for the entire family. Hold on to the kids though!" Derek E. from Park City, Utah.

Down the Chute
The Backdoor Adventure

Down The Chute - The Back Door Adventure is not for the faint of heart. Lube that 50-foot drop chute and get ready for the ride of a lifetime. The rider penetrates the back door dark chute and is immediately immersed in a tight, warm, dark environment. As the riders slide deeper and deeper into the chute, they experience a feeling of euphoria. Due to the size of the chute, riders must go solo. Double penetration is therefore not allowed.

The younger guests generally go back for a second time within a few minutes. The older guests tend to need a recovery period before they try it again. Size limitations apply.

"OMG! Down The Chute was scary the first time, but then it became easier the next few times. It was so tight and dark. I did not see a front entrance so guests entered through thc back door only. Maybe an error by the ride designers? In any event, I loved it!" John D. from Little Rock, Arkansas.

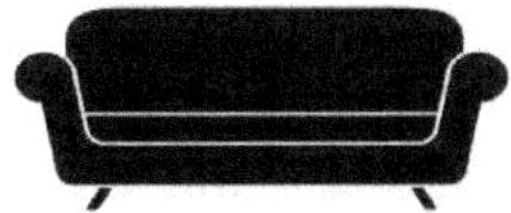

Don’t Tell Anyone Hollywood Adventure

Inspired by the tales of the Hollywood casting couch, the Don’t Tell Anyone Hollywood Adventure is one of the most popular rides in the park. Riders sit in a casting-couch affixed to a rail. Each couch has a picture of one of the accused in the Hollywood “me-too” movement.

The ride creeps slowly along a track through a completely dark tunnel which is filled with a special knock-out gas. Once the rider is semi-conscious, park hosts molest each rider for up to five-minutes. The riders then come to the end of the ride where 100% oxygen is pumped in, waking up the rider.

Guests leave the ride feeling violated but have no idea why. Most guests return to the ride time and time again. Additional oxygen available at the ride’s exit.

Guests under the age of 18 are allowed as long as parental consent is obtained. Winking followed by looking the other way is not considered consent in our park.

“Now I can say I have been to Hollywood! Not once, but multiple times. Words cannot express the thrill of the Hollywood ride. The casting couch car was comfortable. I don’t remember the entire ride but I felt like a star afterwards.” Joan J. from Tulsa, Oklahoma.

“As an aspiring actor, I cannot express my excitement. I love this ride so much that I visited the park office for an application to work as a casting couch host. I just said to myself, ‘hey me too’.” Jodie from West Hollywood, California

The Virgin Scary

It doesn't have to be October to experience the terror of a haunted house. The Virgin Scary, one of the scariest haunted houses on the planet, is open all year around! Guests walk through a dimly lit haunted house. As they enter, they feel intense heat and hear a recording "You are all sinners. If you do not repent, you will burn in Hell". This occurs as 180-degree videos of hell (people burning and screaming) are shown on the walls, complete with special effects. As the guests pass through hell, they are surrounded by priests and nuns who slap the guests with rulers and Bibles.

Another scary section is filled with crying ministers holding empty collection plates. Many clergy guests believed this was the scariest section of The Virgin Scary. The final scene is a depiction of the crucifixion displayed on mirrors. Loud speakers repeatedly play "see what you did to me?" as guests see themselves in the mirrors. The guests are locked in this area for several minutes until the door opens and they are allowed to exit.

Upon exiting the haunted house, a park employee hands each guest a gift card for $5.00 off a crucifix mirror at the gift shop.

“I was peer-pressured into the Virgin Scary Haunted House. I don’t like haunted houses because I am easily frightened. One of the nuns hit me kind of hard with a ruler, which incited a Catholic school flashback and triggered PTSD! That was the scariest part for me. I think the Haunted House entrance should have a trigger warning for those who went to Catholic schools.” Evan W. from Topeka, Kansas.

“As a minister I was horrified by the empty collection plates. I have been in many haunted houses, but this one was the scariest. I will probably have nightmares for years to come! The skyway was awesome.” Pastor Rob, from Cranbury, New Jersey.

Little Man in the Boat

The Little Man in the Boat is an endorphin releasing ride and a ride of exceptional craftsmanship. Guests experience tropical excitement as they tour the Isle of Lesbos. Follow the timeline of the Sodom and Gomorrah saga as you wind through our very own tunnel of love.

Riders sit in a sculpted taco shaped boat which travels along a vibrating track. Hidden in plain sight in the folds of the boat is the little man. The little man is said to bring good luck to those who rub it long enough. Riders may rub the little man in the boat as little or as much as they desire. Some women who dare to experience the ride with their partner express concerns that their partner did not want to rub the little man at all.

"All in all, it was a fun ride, but it was kind of boring and I expected a climax at the end", said Mary Ellen from Little Horse, Wyoming.

“My wife talked me into riding the Little Man in the Boat ride. She kept insisting I rub the little man during the ride, but I didn't. I just don’t believe in it. I enjoyed the Isle of Lesbos presentation.” Mason F. from Eufaula, Alabama.

“We chose to spend our honeymoon at the park. Glad we did! We could not get enough of the Little Man. Our hands and the little man were practically rubbed raw by the end of the day. It brought us considerable pleasure. We can’t say enough good about the Isle of Lesbos exhibit. Thanks Heaven’s Entry! We love you.” Jessica and Mary Ann L. from Carlsbad, New Mexico.

Bun-Jeeesus

Not for the faint of heart. Climb 65-feet up the stairway to heaven. Wait your turn to be strapped into a harness attached to a 50-foot rubber bungee cord. If you love bungee jumping, you will love the Bun-Jeeesus jump. Do it in the name of heaven, do it in the name of the father, the son, or the holy spirit, do it without losing control of your bladder, but just do it!

"Bun-Jeeesus was my favorite. As I followed the stairway to heaven, I had my doubts and struggles. But once I arrived at the staging area I was calm. I saw the sun shining in and I just walked toward the light. It was about that time they shoved my ass off the platform! Loved it so much I jumped (was pushed) three more times!" Christine S. from Missoula, Montana.

"Strap on. Get behind me and push hard. Let's go!" A frequent ride participant. Anonymous.

Dry Beaver

Our resident beaver has been busy building a dam on our lake. The dam is affectionately known as the God dam". Rent a kayak and take a leisurely paddle across Lube Lake and Reservoir to see the natural God dam.

Our beautiful yet introverted beaver has not had a mate during her time in the park lake and frequently stays out of the water. Due to that lack of interaction, the beaver is said to be dry, not wet. However, occasionally the beaver will approach a kayaker and allow petting. If a guest is blessed to pet the beaver, and strokes it just right, the beaver will get wet and excited.

Stuffed beavers (wet or dry) are available for sale in the gift shops!

"For the first time in my life, I was able to pet and rub a beaver. After several minutes of rubbing, it made some peculiar sounds, rolled around, and swam away. Thank you for creating a beautiful park where guests are free to rub the beaver! The God dam was really beautiful and the beaver was soft." Mikal E. from Colorado Springs, Colorado.

"The kayak time was so relaxing. The cutest beaver (el castor) I have ever seen. It was so wet and hairy. I checked Noah's Exotic Meat Diner for beaver but it was not on the menu. I really wanted to eat a moist, delicious beaver after my kayak adventure." Juan from Bacalar, Mexico.

Forty Days

For those who have often longed to have been with Jesus on his 40-day desert experience, the Forty Days is the adventure for you! This adventure simulates 40-days and 40-nights in the desert all within 40-minutes. The machinery and technicians in this attraction are amazing!

The male guide will take twelve men (ages 18+) into the secluded sand pit theater. All participants must sign an agreement not to discuss what happens during their time in the attraction. Also, the men must choose a disciple name and use that name throughout the experience. There is an extra charge for the costumes (long robes and sandals). No drinks or snacks allowed.

Men who share the experience say "WOW, just WOW" and "I was repeatedly filled with the Holy Spirit".

"WOW. Unbelievable! I drew the name Judas so it maybe was not as much fun overall. But it's still well worth being a member of the bro-club for 40-minutes. Better than a man cave on game day." Jake C. from Milan, Ohio.

Lube Land Safe Zone

We understand that sometimes life can be overwhelming. Visiting the park may likewise be overwhelming. For park guests who have suffered micro-aggressions or who are triggered for any reason, we have a place for you! Lube Land Safe Zone is the place to be. The enclosed and private area, filled with hundreds of tropical plants, has hidden speakers that play Jesus inspired comforting quotes. Safe for the kiddos!

Microaggressions and triggers come in many forms and are different for each guest. One example is if a visitor was playing a park game and lost, but did not receive a participation trophy. That visitor could certainly proceed to the Lube Land Safe Zone. James, from San Francisco, a recent park visitor, stated that he went to the Safe Zone when he observed a big man wearing a red shirt.

As James explained "Red is a power color. That big man did not need to wear such a powerful color!". James spent most of his park visit in the Safe Zone. He did eventually enjoy the Lazy River ride.

Holy Trinity Skyway

Our Holy Trinity Skyway connects the adventure of the rides to the park's main restaurants. Painted in our favorite heavenly gold color, the skyway, at its peak, is 100-feet above the park. With its glass floor, it's not for the faint of heart.

As guests walk the first, second, and third loops, they are reminded of the father, son, and holy spirit. The breathtaking design conveys a certain calmness and serenity. Many meditate or pray on the skyway. However, many on the skywalk are heard exclaiming, "Oh Jesus get me out of here!" which tends to negate the serenity of the design.

"I felt so close to God on the Holy Trinity Skyway. Unfortunately, at the highest point I became dizzy and threw-up on some people 100-feet below. Definitely do not walk the Skyway if you are afraid of heights." Agnes W. from Macon, Georgia.

"Our family was having a spiritual time at the park until someone on the Skyway lost their lunch and chunks rained down upon us. It wasn't manna! We had to go to the showers to clean up. The kids were crying." The Smith family from Blowing Rock, North Carolina.

The Restaurants and The Bar

666- The Mark of the Feast

Whether it's a quick pop in and take-out, or sit and enjoy, your trip to the "666" is bound to satisfy your hunger. Our foods are hot and spicy, except for the desserts of course! Choose from our devilishly delicious menu:

- Deviled Eggs
- Deviled Ham Sandwiches
- Deviled Crab
- Hotter than hell Devil sauce
- Satan Salad
- The Devil Went Down to Georgia peach pie
- Devils Food Cake

"All of my life I was taught to fear the number 666. But I have to say, NO MORE! The 666 menu is limited, but the service is great and the food is tasty." Martin Z. from Juneau, Alaska.

The Last Supper

Our guests will be seated at one of the Last Supper (the painting) inspired theme tables, seating for thirteen. Each table must have exactly thirteen guests. Therefore, if your party does not include thirteen people, get to know the neighbor seated next to you!

On the menu is bean stew, lamb, olives, bitter herbs, tilapia with fish sauce, unleavened bread, dates, and aromatized wine. Guests are known to pass bread and wine to their supper mates. Don't passover dessert! Save room for our famous fig infused pudding.

For I was hungry and you gave me food, I was thirsty and you gave me water, I was a stranger and you fed me; all for $59.99.

"I enjoyed the Last Supper Diner. There were only two of us so we were seated with strangers. But we were not strangers for long. Unfortunately, I spilled some sauce on the toes of the guest seated to my right so I washed his feet. Enjoyable and the food was amazing too! I highly recommend this Diner." Mark and Cindy from Minden, Nebraska.

Burning Bush BBQ

Some of the best BBQ in the area prepared by Moses, the smoke pit master. We use only the finest bushes to flavor our meat. Slow smoked to tender perfection. You will want to eat our meat and swallow time and time again. Choose from brisket, pork ribs, chicken, turkey, or sausage. Plenty of sides make for a hearty meal.

All BBQ dishes taste better with our famous Ale Mary beer. It's sweet and sassy!

"I loved Moses' meat. He even asked me to visit his pit and see his raw meat. That was amazing. When I saw his meat, I knew it would soon be in my mouth. His meat filled me up. I had no room for any more. If you visit, try the Ale Mary. It's a great park lager." Tim Y. from Pella, Iowa.

Holy Hell Hotdogs

Our 12-inches will satisfy any appetite. Once your lips wrap around the firm beefy meat, you will want to quickly swallow to savor the taste. Our delicious buns are steamed to perfection in the gates of hell steam tray. Our 12-inch dogs are covered with the devil's red sauce, infused with just a hint of holy water to tame the flame.

Smother your dog with plenty of free fixins. Grab a bag of chips and a soft drink for the full meal deal.

"Best twelve inches I ever swallowed." Britney S. from Hood River, Oregon.

Fellowship Luncheon Diner

Stop by for lunch with fellow park guests. Welcome strangers to your table as you break bread in our modern diner, built to capture the ambiance of a church basement. Sometimes park actors will stop by for some fellowship and a bite to eat. Meet and eat with your favorite actor! Open for lunch only, 11:00am - 1:30pm. Reservations not required.

Not to worry, all of your favorite dishes are on the menu:

- Green bean casserole
- Baked mac & cheese
- Potato salad
- Baked beans
- Fried chicken
- Hot Dogs
- Hamburgers
- Potato chips
- Jello Salad
- Fruit Plate
- Watergate Salad
- Mystery Casserole
- Red velvet cake
- And many more favorites

And what fellowship luncheon would be complete without screaming children? Yes, we hire child actors to run around, ask when it's time to leave, and essentially ruin the luncheon. We also hire some elderly ladies to gossip about the guests to make everyone feels right at home in our after-church service ambience themed diner.

"We truly felt like we were back home in our church basement! The park nailed it! The menu is the same as at any fellowship luncheon. The kids were annoying (well done you young actors!) and the gossip was spot on. We were impressed by the way the elderly ladies would gossip and then laugh. Well played. We are definitely coming back!" Mr. & Mrs. Davis, NYC, New York.

Holy Smoke Cocks & Waffles

Who doesn't love a good cock with their waffle? We use only the finest and biggest cocks, battered and deep fried to golden perfection. Our cocks are free-range and have never been used for fighting. This makes for a more tender and juicy bird. No hens used here. Just ask anyone who has dined at our restaurant.

The meat is so tender that no one has ever choked on our cock while eating it. The juice seems to squirt out with each bite. Ask for our special white dipping gravy on the side. We make unleavened waffles, almost as tasty as Belgian waffles topped with our honey pot syrup.

For those who end their park adventure at the Holy Smoke Cock and Waffles and can't eat all of the food, we'd be happy to wrap your cock for the ride home.

"My favorite food of all time. I thought that only female hens were used. Was I ever wrong! I changed from eating female to male meat once I tasted the cock from Holy Smoke! It goes down easy! It was so delicious. My mouth waters just thinking about that hot steaming cock." Elijah J. from Hancock, New Hampshire.

Noah's Exotic Meat Diner

Noah has a way with meat. He believes that no animal is safe so his staff goes to all ends of the earth to hunt anything that climbs, walks, or crawls. Rain or shine, his crew is out hunting for animals that Noahs can cook up and serve to the hungry guests. Whether it's Bat Soup, one of Noah's favorites from China, or Camel Toe quiche, we have it here at Noah's Exotic Meat Diner.

Our house communion wine pairs nicely with a smoked meat dish. Guests enjoy the Ark themed seating. Ask for our special 2x2 mom and dad special.

"The Bat Soup was delicious and paired nicely with the smoked salmon. I felt the ark-like seating was a bit cramped. We had the 2x2 mom and dad special. We were disappointed that our gay friends were not able to request it though." Tom and Rose Smith from Dorset, Vermont.

Adam's Rib

Short ribs, beef only. No unclean meat served here. Women quickly become a fan of Adam's ribs. Our special is ½ off ribs, ladies only, each Tuesday. Pardon our long wait time as we typically have a skeleton crew working the smoke pit.

Pair your beef with a tempting house blend salad. We will be happy to toss your salad table side! Save room for our heavenly Angel Food Cake.

"I had a taste for pork ribs but I understand the 'clean meat' thing. The cute waiter tossed my salad right at the table! It was amazing. Best I ever had. My partner skipped the salad and over indulged in eating the meat. Great food and memories." Brad and Juan from Fresno, California

"The table side tossed salad was unbelievable! We enjoyed it so much we plan to incorporate it into our home dinner plans." Sean and Dante from Seattle, Washington.

Loaves and Fishes

It is our popular "all you can eat" fish and bread meal. We serve some of the freshest tilapia and tasty bread, baked daily. It seems like a miracle that our chefs prepare limited fish and bread and turn it into an all-you-can-eat feast for up to 5,000 daily guests. Several selections of wine are available for an extra fee. Reservations highly suggested.

"This place was packed. Thankfully we made reservations. No wait staff here. Instead, diners at the front tables pass back the fish and bread until everyone has a plate full. Well, except that one "well fed" guy at the front who didn't pass anything back! Tasty, crispy, and golden fried fish. Choice of bread. Excellent." The Wagners, party of five from Charleston, South Carolina.

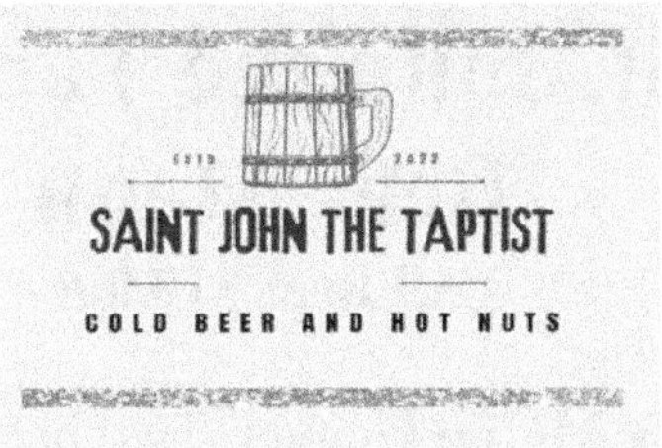

Saint John the Taptist

John, the barkeep, is affectionately known as King of the Brews. Our built upon a rock bar is a haven for guests seeking a cold beer! Quiet and cozy, all guests over the age of twenty-one are encouraged to stop by for a cold brew and some hot nuts (peanuts in the shell). For non-drinkers, our house brewed Virgin Mary non-alcoholic beer is sure to hit the spot. Check out our beer menu for your favorite. Be bold and try a new brew.

Some of the best beer in the world. We drove 600 miles to be guests at the highly acclaimed park! We were disappointed that we could not taste the Foaming Red Sea beer since we missed the five-day period it was served that month. We heard it gives you wings. But the Taptist hooked us up with Father I have Sinned and the Porcelain God beers. Tasty, smooth, and we were blessed with souvenir mugs to take home. Thanks! Great time." The Mullers from Franklin, Tennessee.

St. John the Taptist Beer Menu

(All Beer $10.00)

1. **Take Me To Heaven** Two beers and you will feel like you left the earth.
2. **Father I Have Sinned** Served in a souvenir confessional shaped mug.
3. **Holy Spirit** Blessed by park ministers. Tastes great but less filling.
4. **Lord Almighty** A light ale infused with just a hint of myrrh.
5. **Jesus Juice** A frankincense flavored lager.
6. **Virgin Mary** Non-alcoholic
7. **Porcelain God** Bitter beer served in a souvenir toilet shaped mug.
8. **The Dark Plague** Dark ale made with middle eastern hops and barley.
9. **Halo Hops IPA** Even the saints would cuss if they tasted this ale!
10. **Lott's Lager** Escape the excitement with this higher sodium beer.
11. **Noah's Bark** Flooded with water making it our weakest beer.
12. **Foaming Red Sea** Made from blood oranges giving it a distinctive red color. Only served once a month for five-days.

Services, Shops and Concessions

Amusement parks are not just about the rides and attractions. Guests also want to shop and eat! The park has plenty of shopping, shops, restaurants, diners, concession stands, and snack bars. Want to visit a hair stylist? We have that covered. If a guest is feeling the heat and needs to cool down, how about a snow cone?

Guests are sure to find the perfect personal lube in one of our park stores. Heaven's Entry Lube Park has the most extensive selection of personal lube in the world.

Tease It To Jesus Hair Salon

The higher your hair, the closer you are to heaven. Let one of our experienced stylists design the perfect hairstyle for your day at the park. We can tease it to Jesus, create a more humbling Pentecostal bun, or any style in between. We give good hair jobs.

Tease It To Jesus will expand next season to include the Down Under Salon. The Down Under will feature trims and waxing for a guest's private parts. For men or women. Let us tame your bush.

"I couldn't wait to sit in the chair and let Armando do his magic. After he styled my hair, I had to duck to get out of the salon door. I never felt so close to heaven in my life. Armando does give a good hair job!" Gladys from Provo, Utah.

Be The Face of Jesus – Face Painting

Let the little ones cut loose and express themselves by having their cheeks decorated with their choice of Merry Mary or Jumpin' Jesus. Fun for kids ages two to ninety-two.

"My mother wanted her face painted. She is 78-years young. She had Mary painted on one cheek and Jesus on the other. She really cut loose for her fun day at the park. She later admitted that she felt like Jesus was actually sitting on her face. So cute." Name and city not provided.

Bible It Up Bookstore and Gift Shop

The perfect respite from the fun and sun. Relax and stroll through our park bookstore, full of your favorite books and gifts. Choose from our large collection of Bibles, all sizes, all shapes. All of our trinkets, symbols, idols, and faith-based paraphernalia have been blessed with Holy Lube! Park House band CDs available. (Hablar Espanola) Sorry, no returns.

Fig Leaf Clothiers

Here at "The Fig" we only sell the finest modest garments that any of our guests would love to wear. Most garments are made in-house by local church ladies. No mixed fabrics here. We sell everything from women's one-piece turtle neck swimwear, to black socks for men to wear with sandals. We even sell the sandals!

We didn't forget about the kids. From burning bush panties to choir boy thongs, we have something for everyone. A word to the wise, when we advertise that boy's pants are ½ off, the shop becomes crowded. Wait times apply. Come early and come often.

Ye Old Blessed Lube Shoppe

Let's face it, this is a lube park so we have to know lube. No one does lube like we do! Our team of research scientists and clergy have created the world's best selection of lubes using only the finest ingredients, sourced from all over the world.

Pick the occasion and we guarantee to have the perfect lube for you! Whether alone, with a partner, or with a group, we have you covered (in lube!). Buy three, get one free. Sunday Sunset Lube half off each Sunday. All the lube has been blessed by park ministers. It truly is "holy lube".

- Holy Hole Blessed Lube
- Holy Spirit Water Based Lube
- Very Berry Blessed Feminine Lube
- Blessed Lube (by the church for the church)
- Holy Moses Lube
- Eve's Garden Tropical Lube
- Blessed Trinity Healing Lube (Three lubes in one)

- The Lord Works In Mysterious Ways Apple Healing Lube
- Holy Hole Spirit Plant Based Lube
- Burning Bush Soothing Lube (The only lube used in the park has been hand selected tested and endorsed by ministers)
- ARK (If lube was used on the Ark, it would have been this one!)
- 4-Fingers Blessed Lube
- Sunscreen and Healing Lube
- Lube Of Joy
- Sunday Sunset Lube
- Fellowship Luncheon Fruit Tray Scented Lube
- Choir Boy Novice Pre-Teen Lube
- Sabbath Special Twice Blessed Lube

"Although they are expensive, the various lubes at the Ye Old Blessed Lube Shop are exquisite. I purchased the 12-ounce Choir Boy Pre-Teen Novice Lube for my 12-year-old grandson who just joined the church choir. I picked up an 8-ounce tube of ARK lube just because of the name. I figured that if Noah would have used it…" Clara M. from Lansing, Michigan.

Satan's Apple Bakery Shop

Our very own apple pie and all things apple bake shop. Go ahead ladies, order one or more of our delicious apple pastries. We don't judge. Eve, our picker, tours only the finest local orchards and hand picks each piece of fruit directly from the tree. She is so tempted to pick more, but we only order small quantities to ensure freshness.

Buy a candied apple to go! Buy two pies and receive a stuffed serpent, your choice of colors. Try our tempting mini-snake shaped tarts; deceptively delicious.

Proudly owned and operated by the Sisters of Mary Have Mercy since 1945. The bakery has been serving the public for years in the local community. We just knew it had to be part of our park and the sisters agreed. Lord have mercy, that's some fine pie!

"OMG! The apple pie at Satan's Bakery is to die for!" Lorina R. from Biloxi, Mississippi.

Latte Day Saints Coffee Bar

Start your day off with a hot cup of coffee, or order a hot cup any time of the day! Or, maybe you prefer your coffee iced? Cold brewed? We have a great selection of your favorite beverages. Choose from the menu or ask our friendly barista to make it your way.

- Cup-o-Teresa. Named for Mother Teresa. This drink is aged and bitter. Add plenty of sugar to make it sweeter. This is our highest priced drink.
- Seventh-Day Espresso. Ask for the Second Coming special and receive a double shot of espresso.
- Mormon Mocca. Salvation in a cup. Steamed milk and whipped cream makes this a favorite of locals and missionaries alike. Be a witness to its amazing taste.
- Jewish Java. Served iced with no extras. This drink is a testament to older times. Not served on Saturdays. We accept tips.
- Christian Cappuccino. If you did not order this your first time here, be sure to order it your second coming. You will be glad you waited for

this coffee event served with a fury of whipped milk foam. It's heaven sent.

- Mass. This hot beverage seems to take forever to make. Guests sit, stand, and kneel waiting for their order. Guests confess that they do not like to wait, but the drink promises to forgive their bad day. Mention your favorite saint and you will be blessed with a shot of caramel syrup.
- Judas Juice - Order your favorite but we will betray you and make a barista's choice. Surprise! Priced right at 30-silver coins (dimes). Tip not included.
- Easter Espresso. This drink is so strong it could wake the dead! Try it, if you want to resurrect your energy.
- Atheist Americano. Watered down Espresso with a splash of Irish cream. If you were not a believer before, a cup of this steaming pleasure will make you a believer.
- Virgin Virtue. Traditional plain coffee affectionately known as "yawn" by your fabulous baristas. Ask for your virgin yawn with or without cream.

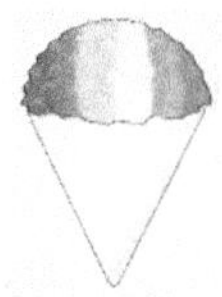

Jesus Wishes He Had a Snow Cone Stand

Hot outside? Refresh and cool off with one of our twelve delicious snow cones, or "raspas"

Our fresh flavors include:

- Mary Berry
- Blue Balls - Double cup of blueberry
- Red Sea – Split down the middle and covered with strawberry sauce
- Holy Hell – Spicy red chili syrup
- Star of Wonder – your choice of syrup, adorned with a candy star
- Amazing Grace Grape (How sweet thou art)
- Hail Mary – served in a football shaped souvenir cup
- Crown of Thorns – blackberry syrup
- Saints Sour Cherry
- Virgin Cherry
- Lucifer Lemon
- Beelzebub Banana

Games and Entertainment

Don't Spill The Seed

In this game men are provided a small container of gelatinous liquid. They run down a track lined with female park employee cut-outs. The first man to cross the finish line without spilling his seed wins! Players are encouraged not to spill their seed on the ground or on the female cut-outs. Seed spillers are eliminated. And remember, don't start until the signal sounds. Premature seed spillers will be shamed and then eliminated. Guaranteed non-stop laughter. Choice of prizes for the winner.

"I was surprised because I thought it was an easy game. I can provide a testament that it was hard the entire time." As shared by Jack, Omar, Reggie, John, Tom, Kevin, Jacob, and Bill.

Glory Hallelujah Hole

Players are seated in one of twelve disciple chairs separated from the other players. Once seated, the lights are turned off. Biblical objects are passed through the glory hallelujah hole; a circular hole cut into the wall. But be careful, not all objects will be based on the Bible! It's always a surprise what may pop through the hole. Players buzz in once they think they know the object.

Scores are tallied and the winner is announced when all players leave the gaming area. The winner receives a trophy depicting a small wall complete with a circular hole cut into it. The words "I won the glory hallelujah hole challenge" are embossed on a heavenly golden back plate.

"I proudly display my glory hole award on my mantle. I felt things I had never felt before. But through divine intervention, I won the prize!" Anonymous

Nuns on the Run

Players enter a convent inspired paint gun gallery wearing Pope garments. In the gallery, moving nun targets randomly pop up. Players shoot the nuns with paint pellets shot from the rapid-fire paint guns.

The attached peanut shooting gallery offers the same entertainment but the little tots hit the nuns with over-sized rulers. (Many players said they enjoyed turning the tables by being able to strike a nun with a ruler!)

Be sure to take home our Nuns on The Run board game. Fun for all ages. Available in the gift shops.

"We played the game (and lost) but it was a blast. We bought the home game for family game night. I'm sure it will provide many laughs!" The Cardenas family from Marfa, Texas.

Donkey's Delight

Guests enter a 180-degree dome theater and sit in one of the 100 seats which replicate real-life donkeys. The guests delight in the story of Jesus' birth as it is projected around them at 180 degrees. Fans blow wintery cold air and the donkey seats move with the action on the screen.

Won't you come along on the journey as Mary rides Joseph's ass all the way to Bethlehem? This spectacular 180-degree replication (and in 3D) can only be seen at Heaven's Entry Lube Park! A must see for the entire family. Critics rave about the authenticity.

"I must say, this is the first time I sat on a donkey. It felt real. At some point I believed I was riding Joseph's ass. The adventure was so realistic. The dome audience became very quiet when Mary screamed during labor." Lulu and Ted from Bangor, Maine.

So Help Me God Mystery Theater

In this intimate dinner theater, twenty guests will reserve a seat in our park production of Who-Dunnit. Ten Ministers spend the show in the company of a couple of 12-year-old male actors. During the course of the dinner and dessert, guests search clues to determine which minister molested which of the underage boys. The acting is superb! This is definitely not Colonel Mustard in the kitchen with a wrench.

For our dinner menu, we start with mini-wiener appetizers, followed by creamed soup, hand rolled tube steak, zippered peas, spinach balls, and wild rice. Served with water, sweet Asian tea, and our exclusive "It's Our Little Secret" red wine. Save room for our tiny rosebud tarts!

"I guessed the molester right away. It only took me five clues. The meal was amazing. I do enjoy a tasty rosebud tart. Each time I eat one I feel like it's my first time." Anonymous

Three Wise Men

Do you have the Bible knowledge it takes to compete? If so, sign up for a slot in our very own version of park Bible Jeopardy. Three contestants will compete in an answer and question game based on Holy Bible knowledge. Each game is played in front of a studio audience! The answer is, *What Bible character saw a burning bush and then decided to become a gynecologist? "Who is Moses?"* It's just that easy!

Sign-up sheets are available in our various gift shops. Want to know what you will be playing for? Winners will receive a gift card for $5 off any purchase of $50 or more in any park restaurant. But wait, there's more. Winners will also have their salad tossed, table side, for free at Adam's Rib Restaurant (A $10 value).

Will you become our idol? Step right up and be tested on your Bible knowledge. Games played at 1:00pm and 3:00pm daily

Carnival Games

No amusement park would be complete without an arcade filled with carnival games. Guests try their luck at winning fantastic prizes at one of the park's many games.

Hail Mary - Guests receive three footballs. The object is to throw a football through the center of a target, twenty feet away. It's not as easy as it sounds though. Throw one ball through the hole and win a rosary. Two or more direct hits score a rosary and a 12-inch ceramic Blessed Mary Mother statue.

Pope On a Rope - In this game, guests are provided with a lasso and are allowed three attempts to lasso a stuffed 18-inch pontiff. If the guest is successful, they will secure the pope on their rope and take their prize home.

Priests Drop - Prepare to take aim! Guests are provided with an air rifle. Sneaky priests fall from above, jump from below, or slip in from the side. Guests never know when a priest will surprise them! Points scored for direct hits on the father's reaching hands. Fabulous prizes for winning this game.

Nun Fun Run- This game combines the power of water jets with the excitement of a hundred-yard dash! Guests are given a water pistol which they must aim at a target hole 10-feet in front of their station. The more water that enters the hole, the faster their nun runs. The first nun to cross the finish line and enter the convent wins! Ten nuns per race, but only one winner.

Nativity Claw- Guests pay for two minutes at the controls of a mechanical claw. In the showcase play area is a nativity scene, complete with camels and all of the usual characters.

Claw and hold onto any of the characters, win that prize! Will you claw baby Jesus or one of the wise men? Claw a camel or cow? Hold onto one of the wise men and take him home for life!

In The Name of The Father - Floating plastic priests follow each other around a lube chute. On the backs of each priest is a letter. Guests are allowed to pick up six priests. If the letters spell F-A-T-H-E-R they win!

Easy and fun for all ages. Game attendants will assist the dyslexic.

Rub One Out - Get your dominant hand ready for the rub of a lifetime. Guests purchase a ceramic idol covered with a latex coating. Rub, rub, and rub until the idol spits out a prize ticket. Some guests switch hands. Do whatever it takes to win that prize. Game side lube provided.

JO - You will never want to JO alone again after you play this game with others. JO, or Joining Others, is a fast-paced group game played with attached joysticks attached to a circular pit on the ground.

Groups of six stand in a circle above the pit and vigorously jerk their movement sensitive joysticks. The winner is the first one to jerk vigorously enough to open a floodgate. The open floodgate allows the lube to flow in the pit section of the fastest player, indicating the winner. Affectionately nicknamed the "circle jerk" by our regular players.

The Isle of Lesbos - This Greek themed game is oddly satisfying. Players receive 100 marbles which they throw one or more at a time, toward the playing area. The playing area has mechanical sheep that munch on a carpet of grass. The more marbles that hit the target, the more excited the sheep become and the more grass carpet the ewe eats.

The object is to sink the most marbles in your target in the quickest time. That causes your sheep to munch all of your carpet and you win! Do ewe have what it takes? Prizes are limited to Birkenstock sandals, all styles, sizes, and colors.

Holy Lube Cornhole Toss Off - Throw one-pound corn cob shaped bean bags twenty-feet across the cornhole staging area. The object is to slam your cob into a pre-lubed holy hole to score points. If you have never cornholed before, now's the time. Cornhole with friends or strangers. Either way, prepare to toss one off with our lubed game. Score points, win prizes!

The Three Crosses - It's our take on the classic game pin-the-tail-on-the donkey. Guests stand in front of three crosses and are handed a velcro backed Jesus figurine. The game starts when the player is blindfolded. Jesus in hand, the player makes three attempts to stick Jesus to the middle cross. Hilarity ensues! Pin Jesus within three tries and receive a Jesus lapel pin prize.

Theater Shows

JJM The Musical Revue

The Manger Auditorium features our house band ("JJM") in the Jesus, Joseph, and Mary Musical Revue.

Our house band plays three shows a day, six days a week. Singing, dancing, joking, and Biblical sketches. See the show program for details. Dark each Sunday.

The last song of every show is heavy metal, JJM's choice. Guests are encouraged to lube shower at one of the theater lube stations and join the slippery SPJ-MOSH pit during the final song. (SPJ - Slippery Praises for Jesus.) Slippery fun, slammin and jammin! No children please.

Jesus, Joseph, & Mary Musical Revue
PROGRAM

SONGS

- My Body is a temple; I'm always open
- Jesus, Joseph, and Harry. A tribute to that special time in the Roman Bathhouse.
- But Father, isn't that a sin?
- Eve was allergic to fig leaves
- We could have picked a pear instead

COMEDY SKETCH

I Hid the Little Drummer Boy's drum sticks

DANCE NUMBER

Jesus leads the 12 disciples in a line dance - a Tribute to Billy Ray

BREAK

SONGS

- The Garden of Sweden (a tribute God's Alps)
- My twelve best friends
- I hate these f*&%ing sandals

COMEDY SKETCH

All of the animals in the manger misbehave!

FINAL DANCE

Ten Lords a leaping are accompanied by eleven pipers piping and twelve drummers drumming. This is a spectacular dance number. The Lords are amazing, the pipers' sweet music sounds like the voices of angels, and the drummers are impeccable.

JJM'S MOSH PIT!

Mary Magdalene Theater – Burlesque Show (18+ only)

What Biblically themed lube park would be complete without a burlesque show? Our very own Mary Magdalene theater actors recreate the ambience of strip clubs from long ago. Audience members are encouraged to dance along to the participation number, "My Body is a Temple, Parking in the Rear".

Touching of the actors is not permitted. Tips allowed in the collection plates. (Partial nudity) 18+.

Bible Thumper Beats

The park hired the best drummers and cloggers for this one-of-a-kind show. Join us in the Thumpers Coliseum and tap your toes to the beat as the performers reenact scenes from the Bible. Watch out for the Parting of the Red Sea number; guests just may get wet! Shows daily at 7:00pm. Black Monday.

Testimonials

"I was called to come here. Not by the Lord, but by my cousin Jenny in Kansas. I have never seen anything like this. I really enjoyed the Holy Roller Coaster. I'm a little sore but I am okay to suffer for my Lord and Savior. It took all of my life savings to attend, but it was well worth the memories I will cherish forever." Beth R. from Muleshoe, Texas

"I thought the Roman Guards were rude. They told me I had to buy a fig leaf shirt or leave the park. Apparently my opaque shirt was too revealing. One of the guards must have skipped leg day at the gym. I was not impressed with his chicken legs. Bless his heart." Robin E. from San Francisco, California

"I felt really hot and went to the park clinic. The church ladies told me to lose weight and then sold me a bottle of cold water. I felt better after I drank some of it. Thanks to everyone for a fun day at the park!" Lee M. from Springfield, Missouri.

"I spent a couple of hundred dollars experiencing the carnival games. But look, I have a stuffed serpent! Well worth the price. Good time at the games and on the rides." Walter L. from Madison, Indiana.

"Fluffy loved the Heavenly Paws pet resort. When it was time to go, we had to drag his ass out of the resort. Definitely coming back." Rachel from Cahokia, Illinois.

Epilogue - Park Revelation

Sunlight shone through the blinds and fell upon Enya's closed eyes, waking him. He stretched as he looked around, laughing lightly as he recalled his dream. Really? A heavenly inspired lube park? Crazy dream, he thought, but it could possibly be an idea for a book.

Enya picked up his phone. "Hey Justin, you will not believe the dream I had last night!"

Enya and Justin met later that day. They began working on a rough draft of a humorous book about, of all things, a Bible themed lube park.

Just For Fun

Ok, so you made it through the book. How many puns did you recognize? Double entendres, jokes? Or maybe you recognized stories from the Bible? Just plain funny? Re-read the book and try to keep count! Challenge your friends and compare scores. Fun for all!

Scores

__________ Puns

__________ Double Entendres

__________ Jokes

__________ Bible Stories

__________ Plain Funny (i.e. "Heavenly Paws")

The Legal Page

What book would be complete without a disclaimer page? So, here it is!

Disclaimer

This is a work of fiction. Names, characters, businesses, places, events, locales, and incidents are either the products of the author's imagination or used in a fictitious manner. Any resemblance to actual persons, living or dead, or actual events is purely coincidental.

Final Joke

After editing, and re-editing, I unfortunately came up a page short of sixty-nine.

I'm sure you will indulge me then as I create this one last page of essentially, nothing. Well, nothing that is, except for one final joke.

69-acre park, $69.00 admission, and 69-pages. We all have that special place in our hearts for the number 69.

Don't forget to add this to your just for fun score!

www.ingramcontent.com/pod-product-compliance
Lightning Source LLC
LaVergne TN
LVHW010501160826
845677LV00012B/2588